D1402581

# Bob the Builder

## THE FUN IS IN ! GETTING IT DONE

Bob the Builder
3 DISCS
Bob's THREE JOBS

Born to Play

mV

Bob the Builder BUILT TO BE WILD
THE MOVIE!
NEVER SEEN ON TV

A wide range of Bob the Builder product available now at all good retailers.

www.bobthebuilder.com

© 2007 HIT Entertainment Limited and Keith Chapman. All rights reserved.

HiT ENTERTAINMENT

# This Bob the Builder Annual belongs to

.............................................................

# Bob the Builder™

## PROJECT BUILD IT

# ANNUAL
# 2008

# Contents

Stories adapted from original scripts by Sarah Ball, Rachel Murrell, Simon Nicholson and Marc Seal.

Based on the television series Bob the Builder © HIT Entertainment Limited and Keith Chapman 2007
With thanks to HOT Animation.

Text and illustrations © 2007 HIT Entertainment Limited.
The Bob the Builder name and characters and the Wendy, Spud, Lofty, Roley,
Muck, Pilchard, Dizzy, Scoop, Scrambler, Benny and Jackaroo characters are trademarks
of HIT Entertainment Limited. Registered in the UK. All rights reserved.

HiT entertainment

**EGMONT**
*We bring stories to life*

First published in Great Britain 2007 by Egmont UK Ltd
239 Kensington High Street, London W8 6SA

All rights reserved. No part of this publication may be reproduced, stored in a retrieval system, or transmitted,
in any form or by any means, electronic, mechanical, photocopying, recording or otherwise,
without the prior permission of the publisher and copyright owner.

ISBN 978 1 4052 3171 8
Printed in Italy
1 3 5 7 9 10 8 6 4 2

# Bob the Builder™

## PROJECT: BUILD IT

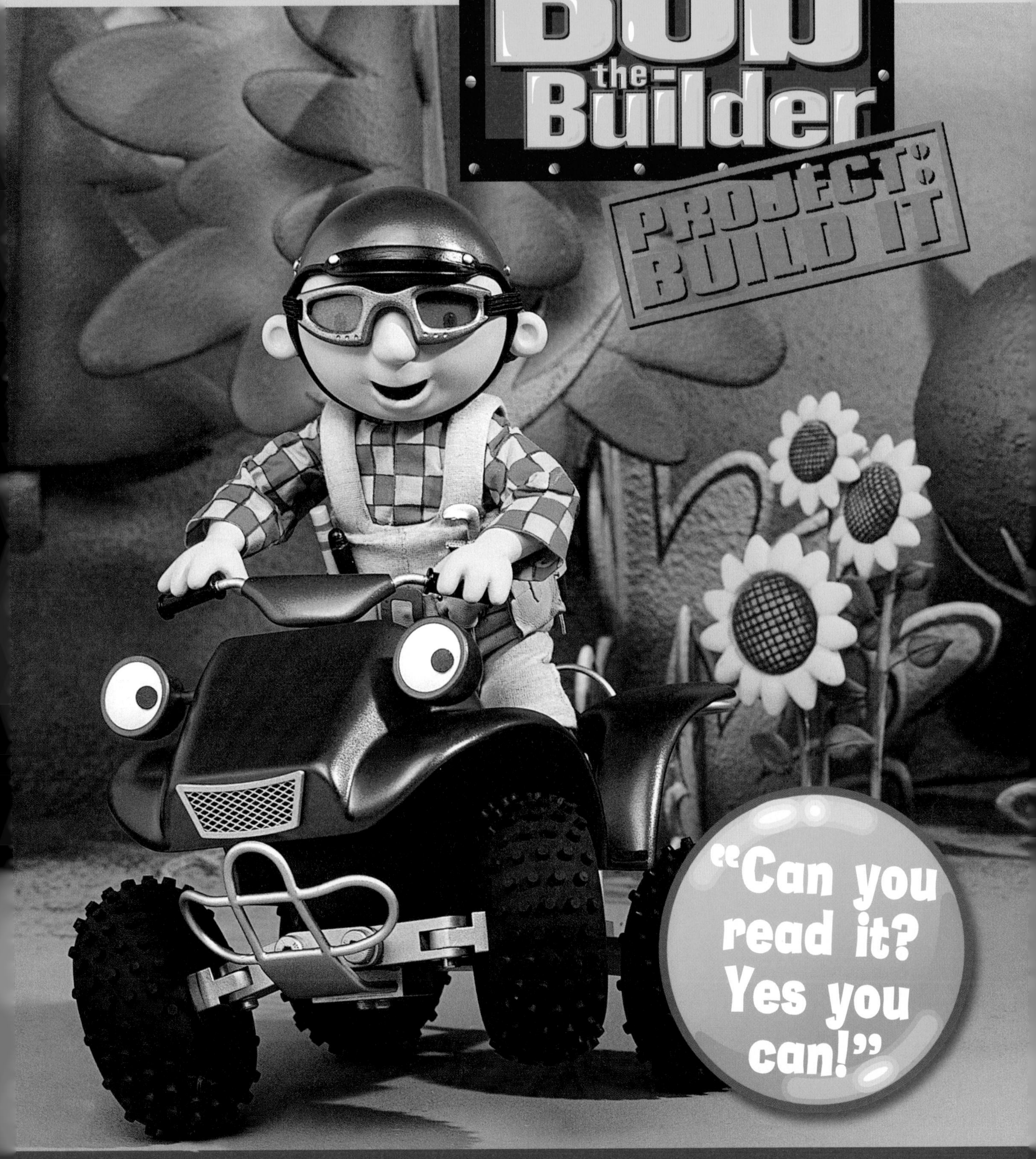

# The story of Sunflower Valley

"When it's finished Sunflower Valley will be a whole new town. It's going to be a very special place that won't spoil nature, and the hills, fields and forests. People will live and work in 'green' houses, and there will still be lots of space for animals, birds, trees and flowers.

"I won the competition to design Sunflower Valley, and now I have to build it! It will be hard work, but I have Wendy and my very special machine team to help me. Working together, we'll get the job done!"

"Can we build it?"
"Yes we can!"

"There are three important words to help us build Sunflower Valley. They all begin with the letter **r**, so they're easy to remember!" Bob tells his team.

"1 **reduce**  the effects of building houses and roads on the countryside

2 **reuse**  as many things as possible, like wood and bricks

3 **recycle**  as many things as we can!"

# Sunflower Valley people

**Bob** has moved from Bobsville to a new yard in Sunflower Valley. He lives in a mobile home with his pet cat, **Pilchard**.

Bob's mum and dad, **Dot** and **Robert**, are looking after the Bobsville yard. They come to visit.

**Wendy** lives in a little caravan with a garden and a vegetable patch. She has a little house for her hens, **Henny** and **Penny**.

**Farmer Pickles** grows sunflowers to make sunflower oil. He lives in a house made of straw bales called Scarecrow Cottage, with **Spud** the scarecrow and his puppy, **Scruffty**.

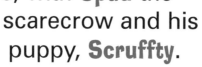

**Mr and Mrs Bentley** moved to Sunflower Valley to live in a special house-in-a-hill.

**Mr Beasley** lives in a round canvas house called a yurt.

# The Sunflower Valley machine team

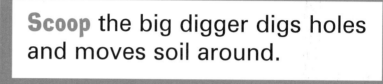

**Scoop** the big digger digs holes and moves soil around.

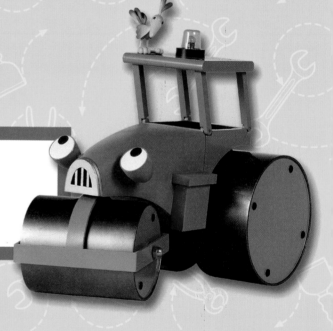

**Roley** the steamroller rolls earth smooth and flat. His friend **Bird** sits on his cab.

**Dizzy** the cement mixer mixes cement and plaster in her tub.

**Muck** the digger-dumper digs, dumps and moves earth around.

**Travis** the tractor carries all sorts of things in his trailer.

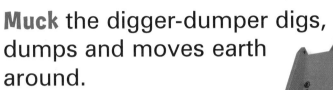

**Lofty** the mobile crane lifts things in his big grabber.

**Benny** the robo-digger digs and hammers and shovels earth.

**Scrambler** the four-wheel-drive vehicle can work on rough ground.

# Scrambler in the doghouse

It was a sunny day and Bob and Wendy were working in the Sunflower Valley yard.

"I'm glad we've got a break from building today, Wendy," said Bob. "We need a good tidy-up!"

Just then, Farmer Pickles arrived with Scruffty.

**"Ruff! Ruff-ruff!"** said Scruffty.

"What's he so excited about?" asked Wendy.

"I've promised him a new kennel," said Farmer Pickles. "Will you and Bob be able to build it?"

"Yes, we'll do it later this afternoon," said Wendy.

"You can help, Scrambler," said Bob. "I'll load your trailer with the things we need. You can bring them to Scarecrow Cottage later."

"No problemo, Bob!" said Scrambler. "I'll take them after I've been off-roading with Scruffty."

Spud liked the sound of that! "Can I come?" he asked.

"Yeah, wicked!" said Scrambler. **"Ruff!"** said Scruffty.

Spud picked up an old pan and put it on his head as a crash helmet. "Let's go!" he said.

Bob and Wendy took Scoop and Muck to collect unused materials.

"Can we clear it?" said Scoop.

"Yes we can!" said Wendy and Muck.

Down by the river, Spud threw a stick for Scruffty to chase. When he brought it back a beaver was holding on to the other end!

The beaver dived into the water with the stick. "Let's follow him!" said Scrambler.

The beaver had used branches and bits of wood to build a dam across the river.

"Wicked!" said Scrambler.

"Ruff!" said Scruffty. He wanted to go off-roading!

"Right, we'll go now," said Scrambler. "Bye, Mr Beaver!"

Scruffty sat on Scrambler and they raced down a steep hill. Then Scruffty jumped out and leapt into the air from a high bank.

"Scruffty's the best off-roader!" said Spud.

"Better than me?" said Scrambler. "No way!"

"Prove it!" said Spud.

"I will," said Scrambler. "But I need a ramp."

Scrambler and Spud looked for

things to build a ramp with. But Bob and the team had taken everything away!

"I know," said Scrambler. "We'll use the stuff Bob gave me for Scruffty's kennel!"

"Yeah, we build the ramp, then when Scrambler's jumped, we un-build it!" said Spud.

When the ramp was ready Scrambler raced towards it. But – **crash! smash!** – the wood cracked and broke into pieces!

"Oh, no!" said Scrambler. "Now what are we gonna do?"

"You'll just have to tell Bob what you've done," said Spud.

Scrambler took Spud and Scruffty to Scarecrow Cottage.

"What happened?" asked Bob when he saw the broken wood.

"Sorry," said Scrambler. "I … er … needed a ramp … and it broke …"

Just then Scrambler saw the old

stuff in Muck's dumper. "I've got an idea!" he said. "You can use the leftover bits and pieces to build Scruffty's kennel."

"Brilliant!" said Bob. "What do we say, team?"

"Reduce! Reuse! Recycle!"

Bob made the base of the kennel. Then Wendy used old tyres cut in half to make a roof.

"Ruff-ruff-ruff!" said Scruffty.

He loved his new kennel! He gave Scrambler a big sticky lick to say thank you!

"Thanks, Scruffty!" said Scrambler. "Bob and Wendy are the best kennel-builders!"

"And you and Scruffty are the best off-roaders!" said Bob.

"Yay!" said Scrambler.

"Ruff!" said Scruffty.

# Reduce! Reuse! Recycle!

Bob and the team know how important it is to reduce waste, and to use things again. It's the 'green' way to do things and look after our planet.

Make sure you recycle as many things as you can at home and school.

Can the things on this page be recycled or reused?
Write a tick ✔ for yes or a cross ✘ for no in each box.

ANSWER: All the things can be recycled or reused.

21

# Benny's important job

Bob and the team were building a special house for Mr and Mrs Bentley. It was a house-in-a-hill!

Benny wanted to help. "What's my big, important job?" he asked Bob. "Digging?"

"No, Scoop and Muck will do the digging," said Bob. "Then Dizzy and I will make concrete blocks for the walls. Mr Bentley has the plans."

"Let's get started," said Scoop. **"Can we build it?"**

**"Yes we can!"** said the others.

All except Benny. He didn't have a job to do.

Scoop and Muck dug into the hill. They took off strips of grass and soil and Bob rolled them up. Then Dizzy and Bob went off to make the concrete blocks.

Benny looked around. "Can I help Scoop and Muck with the digging, Mr Bentley?" he asked.

"Well, it's a job for big diggers really," said Mr Bentley. "But the house has got to be ready as soon as possible, so you can help them. A photographer's coming to take pictures for the cover of Gorgeous Homes magazine."

Benny dug his digger into the ground. But the earth was very hard and it bounced off.

"Oh," he said. "This job is much harder than I thought …"

Benny dug as hard as he could. But it was no good. His part of the hole was much smaller than Scoop and Muck's.

He tried to think of another job he could do. "I'll mix the concrete," he said.

"Don't be silly," said Dizzy.

"Diggers can't mix concrete!"

She was right. "OK," said Benny. "I'll bring the other things we need."

"No, I'm doing that with Mr Bentley," said Wendy.

Everyone had a job to do. Everyone but Benny. There was still no job for him …

Roley flattened the ground. Bob, Wendy and Mr Bentley put wood in the hole to hold the soil. They built the walls and Dizzy made the floor. Then Lofty brought wood for a frame.

Benny could only watch them work. He felt useless. There was still no job for him to do …

Lofty put the roof in place then he brought window frames and doors. Bob and Wendy covered the roof with rolls of grass.

"Nobody needs a little digger like me," said Benny sadly. "I'm no use at all."

Just then Mrs Bentley and Scrambler arrived. His trailer was full of plants and flowers for the garden.

"How long will it take to plant them?" asked Mr Bentley. "They need to be planted before the photographer comes! There's a lot of digging to do!"

"We'll do it," said Muck. "Me and Scoop."

"But you're both too big to go up the hill," said Wendy.

"But I'm small enough!" said Benny. "Please let me do the digging! It can be my big, important job!"

"OK, Benny," said Wendy.

Benny zoomed up and down the hill. He dug little holes for the plants, dropped them in, then patted down the soil.

He worked really hard. He finished the garden just before the photographer arrived.

"Wow!" said the photographer. "This house-in-a-hill is gorgeous!"

"Thank you," said Mr Bentley. "But I couldn't have done it without Bob's building team. Especially little Benny!"

"Cool!" said the photographer. "I'll take a shot of Benny with you in front of the house. OK, everyone … smile!"

Benny smiled an extra big smile. He was very proud of his big, important job!

# Muck's picture puzzle

Which of these pieces will complete the big picture on the next page? Copy them into the spaces and colour them in.

**1**

**2**

**3**

**4**

ANSWER: Pieces 2, 3 and 5 complete the picture.

# Colour and count with Dizzy and Spud

"Farmer Pickles grows lots and lots of lovely sunflowers. We take the seeds to the factory where a big machine makes them into sunflower oil!"

"It's my job to stop Squawk and the other crows eating all the sunflower seeds. Sunflower Spud, that's me!"

Look at the picture on the next page. How many sunflowers can you see growing in the field behind Squawk? Colour in a sunflower outline for each one you can see. Then count the ones you have coloured, and circle the number.

1 2 3 4 5 6 7 8 9 10

ANSWER: There are 8 sunflowers.

# Bob the Builder

## BUILT TO BE WILD

### part 1: Cactus Creek

Bob and the team were on a Wild West cowboy holiday in Cactus Creek!

Muck was very excited about it. "I'm going to round up cattle and pan for gold," he said. "I'm going to have a big adventure 'cos I was Built to be wild!"

A blue pick-up truck called Jackaroo took them to the Double R Ranch. The owner was called Rio Rogers.

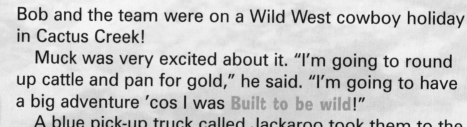

"Howdy, folks," said Rio. "I reckon it's time for y'all to have yer first cowboy lesson!"

Bob changed into his cowboy outfit and sat on Rio's horse, Dollar.

"Giddy up!" said Rio, and Dollar took off.

"Whoa!" said Bob. "Where are the brakes?"

Next, Rio took them into the desert to learn how to use a lasso.

"Dang it!" she said. "I left the rope back at the ranch. I can't teach ya to throw without it!"

"I'll get it, Rio!" said Muck.

"I'll show ya the way!" said Jackaroo.

"I'll help!" said Spud.

"Jump on, pardner!" said Muck.

Jackaroo showed them Cactus Creek and the old gold mine. "Rio's great-great-granpappy Rusty used to live here," he said. "No one lives here now. When the gold ran out, everyone left."

Spud found an old sheriff's badge and pinned it to his waistcoat. "Howdy!" he said. "I'm Sheriff Spud."

"I'll be your horse," said Muck. "Neigh! Clippetty-clop, clippetty-clop!"

Muck raced along the main street. He was having so much fun that he didn't look where he was going and ran into the old saloon. He knocked it down!

The saloon fell over and all the other buildings fell down, like dominoes!

"Oh, no!" said Muck.

Just then Rio and the others arrived. "What happened?" asked Rio.

"Sorry," said Muck.

"Don't worry, Rio," said Bob. "We can fix everything.

I've got the best building team in the world."

"Can we fix it?" said Scoop.

"Can ya?" said Rio.

"Yes we can!" said the others.

All except Lofty. "Er ... yeah ... I think so," he said.

"We'll make things as good as new, Rio," said Muck. "I promise!"

"Why, thank ya," said Rio. "Y'all are the nicest folks I ever did meet!"

Bob, Wendy and the team worked hard all day.

It was dark when they got back to the ranch.
After supper Rio told them about the gold mine.
"They do say ma great-great-granpappy hid some
gold. I'd sure like to find it!"

Will Muck have an adventure? Will Rio find the gold?
Find out in part 2 of Built to be wild on page 40.

# "Yeehaa!"

"Howdy pardners! Can ya find the picture of my pal Rio that's the odd one out?"

1

2

4

3

38

ANSWER: Rio number 2 is the odd one out.

"Which two pictures of Rio's pick-up truck, Jackaroo, are just the same?"

**1**

**2**

**3**

**4**

"Did ya find 'em? Ya did? Yeehaa! Here's a sheriff's badge for you. Write yer name on it, ya hear?"

ANSWER: Jackaroo 1 and 4 are the same.

.........................

# Bob the Builder

## BUILT TO BE WILD

### part 2: Muck to the rescue

Next morning, while the rest of the team was working in Cactus Creek, Rio, Jackaroo, Muck and Spud went to get wood and nails.

"Y'all take it slow," said Rio when they came to an old wooden bridge across the creek.

"I'll walk!" said Spud.

Muck was so excited that he rushed on to the bridge. It creaked and groaned, and one of the ropes snapped, then it rolled to one side!

"Waarghh!" said Muck, rushing across to the other side.

Another rope snapped and the bridge – and Spud! – dangled over the creek.

"Aaaaaaargh!" said Spud. "Help!"

"Hold tight," said Rio. "I'm gonna rope ya!"

Rio's rope looped around Spud's waist and Muck pulled him up to safety.

Muck sighed. "Why can't I have an adventure?"

When they got back to Cactus Creek, some of the buildings were already fixed.

Bob asked Muck and Spud to clear out an old barn. But Muck went off to listen to Rio's stories.

Spud was looking around the barn when suddenly a hole appeared in the ground! He climbed down and found himself in a dark mine and lit an old lamp.

Spud sat in a mine cart and pulled a lever. The cart set off deep into the mine! "Heeeelp!" said Spud.

Outside, Muck heard Spud's cry for help and set off to find him.

"Where are we?" asked Muck when he caught up with Spud.

"In the old gold mine!" said Spud.

They tried to find the way out, but rocks blocked the track.

**"Muck to the rescue!"** said Muck.

He moved the rocks away, but a saddlebag fell from a crack in the roof and hit him.

As Spud put the saddlebag in Muck's dumper he saw an arrow on the wall. "This way!" he said. "C'mon!"

Bob was showing Rio the fixed buildings when a big boulder that blocked the entrance to the mine rumbled and shook, and out came Muck and Spud!

They told Bob and Rio about the mine. "Can we go on an adventure now, Rio?" said Muck.

"Are ya kiddin'?" said Rio. "You've had a mighty big adventure already! Ya pulled Spud outta the creek, then found him in the mine, got stuck, got hit on the head, an' found the way out!"

"I s'pose that was an adventure!" said Muck.

He tipped the saddlebag out of his dumper and Rio opened it.

It was full of gold! "Ya found great-great-granpappy's gold, Muck!"

"You'll be famous in these parts now!" said Jackaroo.

"Me?" said Muck.

"Sure!" said Rio. "We'll tell stories about Lucky Muck, the truck that was struck by gold!"

"Yeehaa!" said Muck.

# Cowboy Bob's quiz

"Howdy, folks! Hope ya had fun readin' all 'bout Muck's Wild West adventure! Can y'all answer these here questions 'bout it?"

**1** Was the town where Bob and the team stayed called:
   a. Cowboy Creek,
   b. Cactus Creek, or
   c. Kansas Creek?

**2** What is Rio's second name?

**3** Rio has a horse called Dollar.
True ✔     or     False ✗?

**4** Who found an old sheriff's badge?

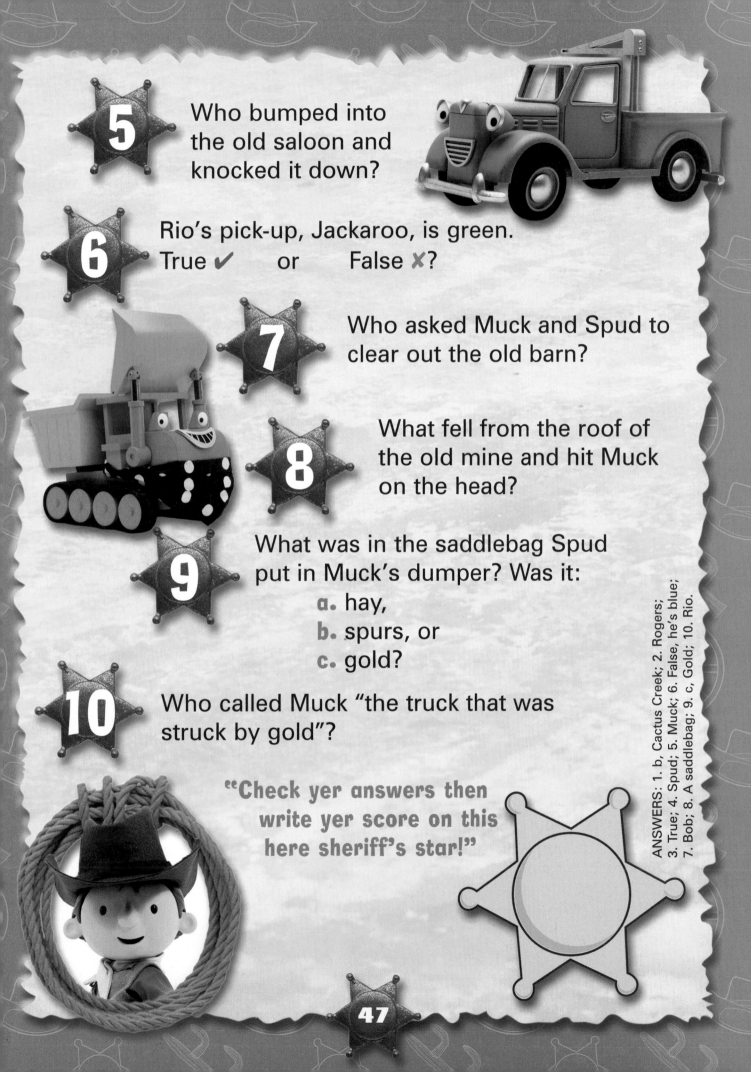

**5** Who bumped into the old saloon and knocked it down?

**6** Rio's pick-up, Jackaroo, is green. True ✔ or False ✘?

**7** Who asked Muck and Spud to clear out the old barn?

**8** What fell from the roof of the old mine and hit Muck on the head?

**9** What was in the saddlebag Spud put in Muck's dumper? Was it:
   **a.** hay,
   **b.** spurs, or
   **c.** gold?

**10** Who called Muck "the truck that was struck by gold"?

**"Check yer answers then write yer score on this here sheriff's star!"**

ANSWERS: 1. b, Cactus Creek; 2. Rogers; 3. True; 4. Spud; 5. Muck; 6. False, he's blue; 7. Bob; 8. A saddlebag; 9. c, Gold; 10. Rio.

# Put-it-together Spud

Spud was scaring birds away from Farmer Pickles' sunflowers when Roley told him that Bob was putting together a machine at the sunflower factory.

"That's something I'm good at!" said Spud. "Put-it-together Spud, that's me!"

Farmer Pickles came to look at his sunflowers.

"Can I go to the factory to help Bob put together the sunflower-oil-making machine please?" asked Spud.

"No, I need you to look after my sunflowers," said Farmer Pickles. "See you later!"

But Spud didn't do as he was told. "Come on," he said to Scrambler. "Let's go."

At the factory Bob and Wendy took the big boxes of machine parts inside.

They didn't see Spud put one of the boxes on Scrambler's trailer and drive off with it!

Spud drove to a field. He opened the box and took out the parts. "That goes there and that must go there …" he said. "The sunflowers go in here … and the oil comes out …"

"What about these other bits?" said Scrambler.

"They go … er … here!" said Spud. "Or there!"

Scrambler was worried about Farmer Pickles' sunflowers. "Spud, you should be scaring the birds, not building a machine," he said.

"I know," said Spud. "Someone else will have to do the bird-scaring for me."

"Who?" asked Scrambler.

"You!" said Spud. "Just do what I do. Off you go. I'm going back to the factory to get some nuts and bolts to hold these bits together …"

At the factory Spud couldn't find the nuts and bolts. So he unscrewed

some from the wall and ran back to the field!

Marjorie, Bob and Wendy looked at the plans for the machine. "One of the boxes of parts is missing," said Bob. "We'd better look for it."

They soon found the parts.

Spud had them!

"Look, Farmer Pickles!" he said. "I made the tank-thingy! I did a good job, didn't I? There's more to Spud than scaring crows!"

Marjorie looked at the tank. "You have put it together very well," she said.

"Yes, yes, yessity-yes!" said Spud happily.

Bob smiled. "Let's take it back to the factory."

But the tank was too big to fit through the factory door!

"We'll just have to take it to bits then put it together again inside," said Bob.

Suddenly they heard a loud noise. **C-r-e-e-a-a-k-k!**

"Look, the wall! It's moving!" said Wendy.

"Run!" said Spud as, **c-r-e-e-a-a-k-k!** the wall fell down!

Spud looked at the nuts and bolts he had taken from the wall. "This is all my fault …" he said.

But Marjorie was smiling. "There's one good thing about the wall falling down," she said. "We can get Spud's tank inside now!"

"Come on team," said Bob.
**"Can we fix it?"**
**"Yes we can!"**
**"Er ... yeah ... I think so,"** said Lofty.

Bob and the team fixed the machine and the wall.

Scrambler arrived with lots of sunflowers. They went into the factory and came out as a bottle of sunflower oil!

"We need lots more sunflowers," said Farmer Pickles.

"I'd better do my job, then," said Spud, jumping on to Scrambler. "I'll scare the birds away. Off we go! Scarecrow Spud's on the job! Shoo, birdies, shoo!"

# Scarecrow Cottage

This picture shows Bob and the team outside Farmer Pickles' new Sunflower Valley house, Scarecrow Cottage. The walls are made of straw bales!

ANSWER: Pictures 2, 4, 6, 8, 9
and 10 are parts of the big picture.

# Two-jobs Travis

Read this story about Travis' two jobs.
When you see a picture, say the name.

**Bob**   **Travis**   **Mr Beasley**   **Farmer Pickles**   **Marjorie**   **Wendy**

 has lots and lots of yogurt pots.

"I'm going to live in a yogurt-pot house,"

says  . "You mean a **yurt** house," says  .

"It comes in this big crate."  asks  to

take the crate to the sunflower field.

 has a job for  too. He asks

 to take trays of sunflower plants to

the field. But  asks  to move

the yurt to a new place near the river.

 works really hard. He gets more

trays for  . Then  asks him

to move the yurt for  again!

calls  on his talkie-talkie.

"  has more plants for you," says

 .  chugs off.  wants

to save time so he takes lots of trays

at once.  goes so fast that they fall

off! "Oh no!" says  . "Sorry,  .

Sorry,  . I was trying to do two jobs.

There's only so much one tractor can do."

"Unless his friends help him!" says  .

"I'll put up the yurt," says 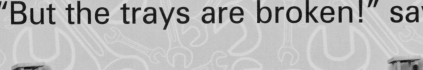 .

"I'll take the seed trays," says 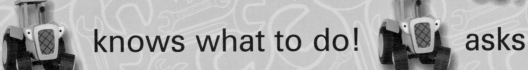 .

"But the trays are broken!" says 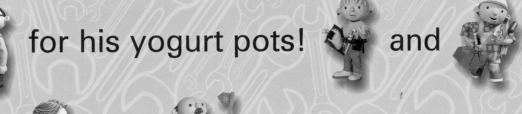 .

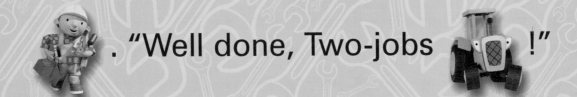 knows what to do! asks

for his yogurt pots! and

and and put a plant

in each pot! takes them to the

field. "Reduce, reuse, recycle!" says

. "Well done, Two-jobs !"

# Mr Beasley's yogurt pots

Mr Beasley collected lots of used yogurt pots! He heard about something called a **yogurt house**, and wanted to build one. But Bob told him it was a **yurt house**, not a yogurt house!

Mr Beasley decided to build a yurt house. It came in a big crate and Bob and the team put it up.

But when the wind blew, some of Mr Beasley's yogurt pots rolled away! He needs to find them to take them to the recycling centre.

# Bob's three jobs

Bob's dad, Robert, was showing the machine team the pictures in his bird-watching book.

"I've seen a few of those … and one of these," he said.

"An eagle?" said Roley. **"Rock and roll!"**

"Dad just loves bird-watching," said Bob.

"Are there any special birds in Sunflower Valley, Bob's dad?" asked Lofty.

Robert showed him a picture of a little yellow bird. "The Lesser

Striped Sunflower Warbler was seen here once," he said. "But it's very rare."

"Bob built a place for watching birdies, didn't he?" said Muck.

"He did, Muck," said Robert. "It's called a hide! Bob and I are going there to do some bird-watching. I can't wait!"

"Right," said Bob. "I've got three little jobs to do first, Dad. I'll see you at the hide."

Bob's first job was to fix a shelf to the wall in Spud's room at Scarecrow Cottage.

Spud had tried to fix it himself, and now there was a huge hole in the wall!

"Oh, no," said Bob. "This is going to take ages."

It did. "Sorry it turned out to be such a big job for you, Bob," said Farmer Pickles.

"That's OK," said Bob. "It's just that I told Dad I wouldn't be long …"

Bob's second job was to fix Mrs Bentley's kitchen window.

It wouldn't open.

"You try opening it from inside, and I'll try outside," said Bob.

"I'm pulling as hard as I can!" said Mrs Bentley.

"No, don't pull," said Bob. "You should be pushing …"

Suddenly the window flew open and the glass cracked.

"I'll fix it," said Bob.

Fitting the new glass took Bob a long time. "I hope Dad's all right on his own ..." he said.

Bob needn't have worried. Robert was busy. A squirrel ran into the hide and he gave it a nut.

Then two rabbits hopped in. "You want some food too, do you?" said Robert. He gave them some lettuce from his lunch box.

Next, two hedgehogs arrived. "News travels fast!" said Robert, giving them some of his apple.

Bob's last job was to put up a radio aerial at Mr Beasley's yurt.

But the aerial was in bits – two big boxes of them!

"It's telescopic," said Mr Beasley. "It fits together like this, then you press the …"

The aerial flipped out, hit the yurt, and ripped a hole in the canvas!

"I'll fix it," said Bob.

He made a patch for the yurt, then fitted the aerial.

"Come on, Bob, let's go to the hide now!" said Scoop.

"Yes," said Bob. "Dad'll be getting fed up."

Robert had been waiting for a long time. He yawned and settled down in his deckchair. "I'll have a snooze before Bobby gets here …"

When Bob got to the hide Robert was fast asleep. "Sorry, Dad …" said Bob.

"Wha-what?" said Robert, waking up. "Oh, hello! You're just in time!"

"Just in time?" said Bob. "But I've left you on your own all day!"

"I've had a lovely time!" said Robert. "It's not often I get to put my feet up these days."

"But look, it's dark," said Bob. "It's too late for bird-watching."

Robert looked out.

"It's just the right time for seeing some birds," he said. "There – see that? It's the Lesser Striped Sunflower Warbler. It only comes out at night!"

# The Sunflower Valley yard

Bob's mum and dad, Dot and Robert, are looking after the Bobsville yard while he's away. When they had a day off, Scrambler took them to Sunflower Valley.

Look at the two pictures of the Sunflower Valley yard. The pictures look the same, but there are 5 things that are different in picture 2. Can you spot the differences?

ANSWERS: 1. There is mud on Muck's cab; 2. A cloud is missing; 3. Dizzy's stripe is missing; 4. A squirrel has arrived; 5. Scruffty has arrived.